Poppy and Max and the Lost Puppy

For Regi
SG

For Darcy, thanks for the tips!
Lindsey x

Reading Consultant: Prue Goodwin,
lecturer in education at the University of Reading

ORCHARD BOOKS
338 Euston Road, London NW1 3BH
Orchard Books Australia
Hachette Children's Books
Level 17/207 Kent Street, Sydney, NSW 2000
ISBN 978 1 84362 392 2 (hardback)
ISBN 978 1 84362 394 6 (paperback)
First published in hardback in Great Britain in 2007
First paperback publication in 2008
Poppy and Max characters © Lindsey Gardiner 2001
Text © Sally Grindley 2007
Illustrations © Lindsey Gardiner 2007
The rights of Sally Grindley to be identified as the author and
of Lindsey Gardiner to be identified as the illustrator of this work
have been asserted by them in accordance with the
Copyright, Designs and Patents Act, 1988.
A CIP catalogue record for this book is available from the British Library.
1 3 5 7 9 10 8 6 4 2 (hardback)
1 3 5 7 9 10 8 6 4 2 (paperback)
Printed in Italy by LegoPrint
www.wattspublishing.co.uk

Poppy and Max and the Lost Puppy

Sally Grindley 🦴 **Lindsey Gardiner**

ORCHARD BOOKS

One rainy evening, Poppy and Max were eating chocolate muffins.

"I love it when it's all wet outside and we're all warm inside," said Poppy.
"I love muffins," said Max.

5

Suddenly, they heard a loud scratching noise.

"What was that?" said Poppy.

"A yip," said Max.

"More like a yap," said Poppy.

"It is coming from outside," said Max.
They looked out.
On the doorstep sat a little puppy.

Yip yap!

"She must be lost," said Poppy.
"We'd better let her in."
Max opened the door. The puppy ran
straight past him and over to Poppy.

Yip!

"She is all wet," giggled Poppy.
"We need a towel."

Max dried the puppy.
"Not too hard," said Poppy.

The puppy licked Poppy's face.
"That tickles," laughed Poppy.

Yap!

"We will have to find the puppy's
owner," said Max.
"Not while it's raining," said Poppy.

The puppy began to whimper.
"She's hungry," said Poppy. "You don't
want this muffin, do you, Max?"
"I might," grumbled Max, as Poppy
fed the muffin to the puppy.

The puppy started chasing her tail.

yip
yap!

"She wants to play," giggled Poppy.
"Give her your ball, Max."
Max threw his ball to the puppy.
The puppy sat on it.

"Throw it back," said Max.
The puppy bounced the ball to Poppy.

Brilliant shot!

"Isn't she clever, Max?" said Poppy.
"It is time she went to bed," said Max.

Max tipped the toys out of his toybox and laid a cushion in the bottom.

The puppy jumped inside, curled up, and closed her eyes.

"Peace at last," sighed Max. "Time for our hot chocolate."
Then they climbed upstairs to bed.

In the middle of the night, they
were woken by strange noises.
A squeak. A boing, boing, boing.
They ran downstairs.

The puppy was bouncing on Poppy's
trampoline with Max's squeaky teddy
in her mouth.

"Brilliant jumping," laughed Poppy.

"Bed," said Max sternly.
The puppy tumbled off the trampoline
and crept slowly over to her box.

"She is just lonely," said Poppy.
"Let's take her box upstairs."
"She is just naughty," said Max.
But they carried the box upstairs and
settled down to sleep again.

When Max began to snore, a wet nose
kissed Poppy's cheek and a warm body
snuggled up beside her.

"Naughty puppy," chuckled Poppy,
but she let her stay.

The next morning, it stopped raining.
"At last. Time to find the puppy's
owner," cheered Max.
"We'll put up a poster," said Poppy.
"I'll do the words, you do the picture."

HAVE YOU LOST
THIS

Max told the puppy to sit still.
The puppy didn't know how to keep
still, but Max was very patient.

scritch
scratch

"Brilliant picture," said Poppy when
Max had finished.
The puppy wagged her tail.

They stuck the picture in the middle
of Poppy's poster, which read:

HAVE YOU LOST
THIS PUPPY?

POPPY AND MAX
ARE LOOKING AFTER HIM AT
MOP COTTAGE
STRAWBERRY LANE.
PLEASE COLLECT.

"Perfect," said Max.
They set off to find the best place
to stick the poster.

There was a tree on the village green.
"That's the best place to
stick it," said Poppy.

"What if the owner doesn't see it?" said Max. "Let's do another one and put it somewhere else."

Brilliant idea!

HAVE YOU LOST
THIS PUPPY

POPPY AND MAX
ARE LOOKING AFTER HIM AT
MOP COTTAGE
STRAWBERRY LANE
PLEASE COLLECT

But on the way home, the puppy
suddenly ran off down the street.
"Come back," cried Poppy.

The puppy leapt into the arms of a little
boy. The little boy was overjoyed.

"The puppy has found her owner,
instead of the owner finding his
puppy," said Max.

"I'll miss her," Poppy said sadly.

"It is good to be just the two of us
again though, isn't it?" said Max.
Poppy gave him a big smile.
"Yes, Max," she said. "It is perfect."

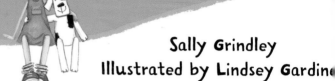

Sally Grindley
Illustrated by Lindsey Gardine

Poppy and Max are available from all good bookshops,
or can be ordered direct from the publisher:
Orchard Books, PO BOX 29, Douglas IM99 1BQ
Credit card orders please telephone 01624 836000 or fax 01624 837033
or e-mail: bookshop@enterprise.net for details.

To order please quote title, author and ISBN and your full name and address.
Cheques and postal orders should be made payable to 'Bookpost plc'.
Postage and packing is FREE within the UK
(overseas customers should add £1.00 per book).

Prices and availability are subject to change.